REBELS

GHOST SHIP

5.102900.862118.000012

001036.10

STAR WARS

Rebel Faction

001000 11 10

8

EZRA'S
WOOKIEE RESCUE

Based on the episode "Spark of Rebellion,"
written by Simon Kinberg

Adapted by Meredith Rusu

Published by Disney • Lucasfilm Press, an imprint of Disney Book Group. No part of this book may be reproduced or transmitted in any form or by any means, electronic or mechanical, including photocopying, recording, or by any information storage and retrieval system, without written permission from the publisher. For information address Disney • Lucasfilm Press, 1101 Flower Street, Glendale, California 91201.

Printed in China

First Edition, December 2014
1 3 5 7 9 10 8 6 4 2

ISBN 978-1-4847-2606-8
T425-2382-5-14356

Visit the official *Star Wars* website at: www.starwars.com
This book was printed on paper created from a sustainable source.

LUCASFILM
P R E S S

Los Angeles • New York

It was a dark time in the galaxy. The Empire had defeated all the Jedi and taken control of many planets.

One planet under Imperial control was Lothal, a tiny farming world on the Outer Rim of the galaxy. A young orphan named Ezra lived there.

Ezra was very clever. He knew how to outwit the Empire's troops and take back the things they stole. Each day he'd bring extra supplies back to his secret tower home on the outskirts of Capital City.

Ezra was stealing supplies one day when he got into trouble. Just as he was about to be captured, a starship appeared and a mysterious rebel named Kanan saved him.

Kanan's ship was called the *Ghost*. On board were four more rebels: Sabine, Hera, Chopper the droid, and Zeb.

Kanan's crew was on a mission to save a transport ship full of Wookiee prisoners.

Ezra protested. He didn't want to go on some crazy rescue mission! But there was no time to take him back to Capital City.

Hera piloted the *Ghost* to the Imperial transport's coordinates. Skillfully, she brought their ship alongside the transport. Kanan, Zeb, and Sabine sneaked aboard while Hera and Ezra remained behind, ready to pilot the *Ghost* out the moment their friends returned.

As Kanan, Zeb, and Sabine crept closer to the transport's brig, a high-ranking Imperial commander named Agent Kallus arrived on board.

What the rebels didn't know was that they were walking into a trap. The Wookiees weren't aboard the transport at all.

On board the *Ghost*, Hera couldn't get a message through to Kanan and the others. She realized the *Ghost*'s transmissions were being blocked. The Imperials must have known they were coming!

Hera spun toward Ezra urgently. "You need to board the transport and warn them!" she cried.

Going to warn the others went against everything Ezra had ever learned about fending for himself. But he realized there was no other choice.

Ezra reached the team just as Kanan was about to open the door to the brig.

Zeb groaned. What was the kid doing there?

"It's a trap!" Ezra cried. "Hera sent me to warn you!"

Suddenly, the brig door slid open, revealing an army of stormtroopers. "RUN!" Ezra shouted.

Kanan, Ezra, Zeb, and Sabine raced back to the *Ghost*. One by one they jumped in through the ship's air lock.

But just as Ezra was about to follow, Agent Kallus grabbed him! "Ah! Let go!" Ezra said.

The air lock snapped shut. The rebels didn't realize Ezra wasn't on board. In a flash of smoke and engine fire, they took off. Ezra had been left behind.

Agent Kallus marched Ezra to a holding cell and shoved him inside.

"Look," Ezra sighed. "I just met those guys today. I don't know anything."

"You're not here for what you know," Agent Kallus said. "You're here to be used as bait upon our return to Lothal."

Meanwhile, Kanan and the others realized that Ezra wasn't with them. Disguising the *Ghost*'s identity signal, Hera piloted it back to the Imperial Star Destroyer that was holding Ezra captive.

Little did they know, Ezra had managed to sneak out of his holding cell! He had nabbed a helmet and was crawling to safety through the ship's air ducts.

On the helmet's intercom, he could hear an Imperial transmission. "I don't know how, but the rebel ship approached without alerting our sensors."

"They came back!" Ezra gasped. "I don't believe it."

Ezra raced to the air lock, where he saw the rebels waiting for him. Sabine held back the stormtroopers with blaster fire while they all jumped aboard the *Ghost*.

The *Ghost* zoomed away from the Star Destroyer.

Hera smiled at Ezra when he entered the cockpit. "Welcome aboard. Again," she said.

Ezra looked at the rebels gratefully. "Thank you," he said. "I really didn't think you'd come back for me." Then he told them something else he'd heard over the stormtroopers' intercom. Something important.

"I know where they're really taking the Wookiees," he said. "Have you heard of the spice mines of Kessel?"

Sabine nodded. "Slaves sent there last a few months, maybe a year."

Ezra looked at each of his new friends. "Then I guess we'd better go save them," he said.

Far away on Kessel, stormtroopers forced handcuffed Wookiees to march into the desert mines. A large laser cannon was positioned on each side of the mine, just in case any daring Wookiees got ideas.

A Wookiee child named Kitwarr reached for his father, frightened. But the stormtroopers yanked him away.

Kitwarr's father, Wullffwarro, growled in anger. He wanted to attack the trooper and protect his son, but there was nothing he could do.

Suddenly, a dark shadow appeared overhead. It was the *Ghost*, coming to the rescue!

Kanan and Sabine used the *Ghost*'s guns to take out the laser cannons. The Wookiees scattered, confused and frightened. Zeb directed them toward the *Ghost*. "Get in, ya furballs!" he ordered. "Now!"

Wullffwarro tried to reach Kitwarr, but a blaster bolt hit him in the shoulder. The dazed Wookiee howled, looking around for Kitwarr. In all the confusion, the little Wookiee had gotten lost!

Ezra realized what was happening and looked frantically for Kitwarr. He spotted him . . . trapped by a stormtrooper on a tall, narrow bridge!

Ezra aimed his energy slingshot at the stormtrooper and knocked him out with three quick blasts! "Gotcha!" he cried, grabbing Kitwarr.

Suddenly, Ezra sensed something behind him and spun around. Agent Kallus was standing at the entrance to the bridge, blocking their path.

Agent Kallus smiled darkly. "It's over," he said.

"Not this time," a voice said.

Both Ezra and Agent Kallus turned toward the voice. Kanan stood atop the *Ghost* as it flew up beside them. And he was holding a lightsaber—the weapon of a Jedi!

Kallus opened fire on Kanan, but Kanan expertly deflected each shot. One blast glanced off Kanan's lightsaber and hit Kallus's shoulder. The Imperial agent staggered backward and fell over the bridge's railing, where he dangled perilously over the pit below.

Ezra and Kitwarr scampered down the bridge and into the *Ghost*. In a blast of light, the ship took off to safety.

On board the *Ghost*, Kitwarr raced into his father's arms. Wullffwarro howled happily. Then he turned to Ezra and Kanan, growling more happy sounds.

"He says if we ever need help, the Wookiees will be there," Sabine translated.

The rebels met up with a Wookiee spaceship that would return the former captives to their homes.

Ezra waved good-bye to his new friends. Then, turning to the *Ghost*'s crew, he said, "Sooo . . . I guess you drop me off next?"

Back on Lothal, Ezra asked Kanan what the Force was.

Kanan smiled. "It binds the galaxy together. And it's strong with you, Ezra. Come with me. You can learn what it truly means to be a Jedi."

A wide grin broke over Ezra's face. To him, that sounded like the best adventure of all.